Dear Parents:

Congratulations! Your child is taking the first steps on an exciting journey. The destination? Independent reading!

STEP INTO READING® will help your child get there. The program offers five steps to reading success. Each step includes fun stories and colorful art or photographs. In addition to original fiction and books with favorite characters, there are Step into Reading Non-Fiction Readers, Phonics Readers and Boxed Sets, Sticker Readers, and Comic Readers—a complete literacy program with something to interest every child.

Learning to Read, Step by Step!

Ready to Read **Preschool–Kindergarten**
• big type and easy words • rhyme and rhythm • picture clues
For children who know the alphabet and are eager to begin reading.

Reading with Help **Preschool–Grade 1**
• basic vocabulary • short sentences • simple stories
For children who recognize familiar words and sound out new words with help.

Reading on Your Own **Grades 1–3**
• engaging characters • easy-to-follow plots • popular topics
For children who are ready to read on their own.

Reading Paragraphs **Grades 2–3**
• challenging vocabulary • short paragraphs • exciting stories
For newly independent readers who read simple sentences with confidence.

Ready for Chapters **Grades 2–4**
• chapters • longer paragraphs • full-color art
For children who want to take the plunge into chapter books but still like colorful pictures.

STEP INTO READING® is designed to give every child a successful reading experience. The grade levels are only guides; children will progress through the steps at their own speed, developing confidence in their reading. The F&P Text Level on the back cover serves as another tool to help you choose the right book for your child.

Remember, a lifetime love of reading starts with a single step!

 Published in the United States by Random House Children's Books, a division of Penguin Random House LLC, New York. Originally published in hardcover in the United States by Penguin Young Readers, an imprint of Penguin Random House LLC, New York, in 2011.

Step into Reading, Random House, and the Random House colophon are registered trademarks of Penguin Random House LLC.

Visit us on the Web!
StepIntoReading.com
rhcbooks.com

Educators and librarians, for a variety of teaching tools, visit us at
RHTeachersLibrarians.com

Library of Congress Cataloging-in-Publication Data is available upon request.
ISBN 978-0-593-43240-2 (trade) — ISBN 978-0-593-43241-9 (lib. bdg.)

Printed in the United States of America
10 9 8 7 6 5 4 3 2 1

This book has been officially leveled by using the F&P Text Level Gradient™ Leveling System.

STEP INTO READING®

MADELINE AND HER DOG

by John Bemelmans Marciano
illustrated by JT Morrow
based on the art of John Bemelmans Marciano

Random House New York

In an old house in Paris

that is covered in vines,

live twelve little girls

in two straight lines.

The smallest one is Madeline.

The girls get dressed

by half past nine.

But Madeline will never leave

without her puppy, Genevieve.

Genevieve sniffs

along the streets,

on the hunt for tasty treats.

A garbage can

is the perfect place

for Genevieve to stuff her face.

Genevieve gets

her dearest wish.

From the river,

she pulls a fish!

“Pee-yew!” say the people
all around.

“That is one dirty,
stinky hound!”

Miss Clavel says,

“We must go right away

and wash this dog

without delay!”

Genevieve thinks,

“Something is not right!”

The pooch puts up a mighty fight.

But she is outnumbered—

that's basic math.

The girls lift her—

SPLASH!

—right into the bath.

They wash their pup
from tail to snout.
As hard as she tries,
she can't get out.

With a rub-a-dub-dub

comes the final

rinse and scrub.

She gives a wiggle

and a great big SHAKE.

Miss Clavel says,

"For heaven's sake!"

The girls pat her dry.

The bath is done.

Madeline says,

“Now wasn’t that fun?”

Genevieve races

for the door.

The girls forgot

to close it before.

In the garden, she digs a hole.

What a perfect spot to roll!

Madeline says,

“Genevieve, no!

Come out right now!”

But the dog won’t go.

At last Madeline

wins the fight.

But she and her dog

are quite a sight!

Now there is a tub for two.

All we need in the bath

is YOU!